D0099849

CAPTAIN BLING'S CHRISTMAS PLUNDER

REBECCA COLBY

PICTURES BY ROB McCLURKAN

ALBERT WHITMAN & COMPANY
CHICAGO, ILLINOIS

’Twas the night before Christmas and all through the ship,
the pirates were planning a plundering trip.
With a spyglass, a map, and a compass to measure,
they plotted a course to steal festive treasure.

Captain Bling steered them north but got caught in a gale
that tossed them and flung them and tore up their sail.

So they followed a light 'til their ship ran ashore,
landing outside Santa Claus's front door.

While peeking through windows, they spied all the elves
wrapping the presents and stacking the shelves.
"Go get that treasure, mates!" Captain Bling cried,
"and heave it on board, for it's nearly high tide!"

B
A

Then Santa appeared, slowly rubbing his eyes—
his nap interrupted by Captain Bling's cries.

And before he could say, “Ho ho ho, what’s that noise?”
the pirates ran off with his treasure of toys!

So Santa gave chase, with his sack on his back,
but the pirates were ready to face his attack.

Though Santa swung fast, the pirates swung faster,
and a sack versus swords was a surefire disaster.

And before he could yell, “Ho ho ho, stop this prank!”
the pirates forced Santa to walk the gangplank.

"Wait!" shouted Santa. "I've checked my list twice,

and chased you to ask if you're naughty or nice.

See, year after year, you've been missed from my list,

and this year I wanted to give you some gifts."

The pirates fell silent; their faces turned red.

Shamed and embarrassed, each one bowed his head.

Overlooked every Christmas, they acted so rotten,

thinking nobody cared...but they'd just been forgotten!

Then Captain Bling spluttered, "Quick, reel Santa in!
And don't harm a hair on his chinny chin chin!"

In the sack there were jewels and gold fit for a king,
and a diamond-trimmed eye patch for posh Captain Bling.

Though thrilled with their gifts and filled with great joy,
they refused to return Santa's treasure of toys.

HELP

Instead, they decided to stow them away,
and kidnapped poor Santa, his reindeer, and sleigh.
And before he could ask, “Ho ho ho, what’s up now?”
all eight of the reindeer were strapped to the bow!

With a flick of the reins, the ship lifted high,
guided by Dasher across the night sky.
Captain Bling spied a chimney, then bellowed, “Ahoy!
Heave-ho and help Santa deliver each toy!”

After scratching his head, Santa Claus understood.

Every one of those pirates had proved to be good!

And before he could say, "Ho ho ho! Help yourselves,"

Captain Bling and his pirates had dressed up like elves.

Now every year since on Captain Bling's ship,
the pirates help Santa prepare for his trip.

And you might hear them call as they lift out of sight,
"Ahoy! Ho ho ho! And to all a good night!"

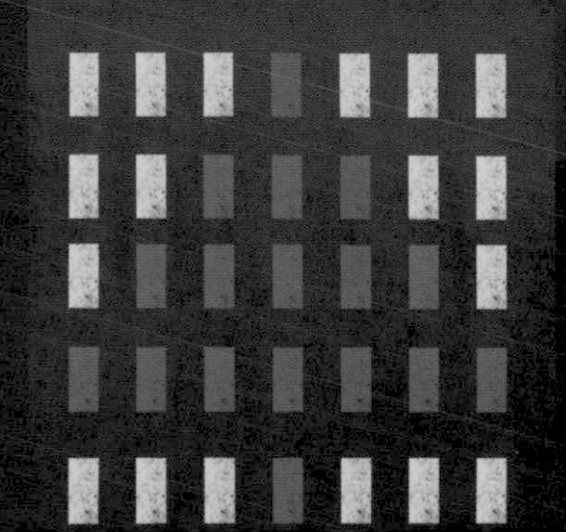

To the PictureBookies who add "bling" to everything I write–RC

For my treasured agent, Anne–RM

Library of Congress Cataloging-in-Publication
data is on file with the publisher.

Published in 2017 by Albert Whitman & Company
ISBN 978-0-8075-1063-6

Printed in China
10 9 8 7 6 5 4 3 2 1 HH 22 21 20 19 18 17

Design by Jordan Kost

For more information about Albert Whitman & Company,
visit our website at www.albertwhitman.com.